The Frog Prince

mitten press

*I*N DAYS OF OLD when wishing still made things so, there lived a king who had three beautiful daughters. The youngest was so lovely that the golden sun itself was filled with wonder whenever it shone upon her face.

*N*ot far from the king's castle was a dark forest. In this forest was an old linden tree, and below the branches of the tree was a cool well.

On warm days, the princess would go into the forest and sit by the well. As she sat, she would toss a golden ball up into the air and catch it. This delighted her in every way, as it was her favorite plaything of all.

One day, her golden ball did not fall into her hand
as she wanted. Instead, it fell to the ground
and rolled into the deep cool well. The
princess watched her ball disappear
and felt very sad. She began to
weep softly, but soon her cries
turned into sobs which grew
louder and louder.

From not far away a voice said, "Why are you crying princess? You sound so sad that even a stone would feel sorry for you."

The princess turned her face to see where the voice was coming from and caught sight of a thick, green frog sticking its head out of the water. At the sight of him she said, "It's you, you ugly old water-splasher. I'm crying because my ball fell into the well."

To this the frog replied, "Be quiet now princess, do not cry. I can help you. But if I do, what will you give me in return?"

The princess said to him, "I will give you whatever you want. You may have my beautiful dresses. You may have my pearls and sparkling jewels. You may even have the golden crown that sits upon my head."

The frog thought about this and answered, "I do not want your dresses, or your pearls and jewels, or your golden crown. If you promise to take me home to be your companion for always, to sit at your table and eat from your little plate, and to sleep in your little bed, and if you promise to love me forever, then I will bring your golden ball back to you."

At this offer the princess simply said, "Yes, I promise. I promise everything."

The frog put his head into the water and dove to the bottom of the well. It was not long before he returned with the golden ball firmly in his mouth.

He tossed it onto the grass and the princess, who was very happy to see her plaything once more, quickly snatched it and ran home.

The frog called after her, "Wait for me, princess, take me with you as you promised."

But the princess ignored his plea and ran home as fast as she could, trying hard to forget about the promise she made to the cold ugly frog.

The next day, as the princess was eating from her little golden plate, something came creeping up the castle stairs with a splish-splash, splish-splash. Then came a steady knock at the door. When the princess saw it was the frog, she slammed the door and ran back to the table.

She tried hard to pretend the frog was not there. But as the frog kept knocking, her face became flushed and her heart began to beat faster and faster. Her father noticed this and asked, "What are you afraid of dear child?"

So she told her father about the frog who rescued her golden ball from the well, and the promise she made to him in return.

*M*eanwhile, the frog started calling,
"Princess, dear princess
please open the door,
for you made a promise
you must not ignore!"
Hearing this, the King ordered his daughter to open the door.
The princess walked slowly and unwillingly to open it for
the frog. He hopped right in and followed at her heels as she
made her way back to the table.

The princess sat down while the frog looked up at her with his big bulging eyes.

"*Princess, dear princess*
with skin white and fair,
now lift me up
let me sit in your chair!"

The princess did not want to do this but she could tell by her father's face that she must not break her promise, so she lifted the frog and let him sit beside her.

ut once the frog was on the chair, he wanted to be on the table. Then once he was on the table he wanted to eat from her little golden plate so he begged,

> *"Princess, dear princess*
> *with hair gold and new,*
> *push your plate closer*
> *so I may eat too."*

The princess did this, but she was not happy. As the frog enjoyed his meal, she could barely eat at all. Every bite seemed to stick in her throat.

Once the frog was satisfied he said,
"Princess, dear princess
with cheeks soft and red,
let us go to your room
where I'll sleep in your bed."

At this, the princess began to cry. She was afraid to touch the cold strange frog. She did not want such a creature in her room or sleeping in her clean and pretty bed. But the king told the princess that she must not scorn the frog who helped her when she needed it.

The princess picked up the frog with two fingers and carried him all the way to her room. Once inside she placed him in a dark corner, turned her back, and went to bed.

As she lay there, she heard something creeping along the floor with a scrip-scrape, scrip-scrape. She looked down to see the frog sitting next to her bed.

"Princess, dear princess
with quilts warm and deep,
lift me up to your bed
where you said I would sleep."

The princess became furious over having to share her room and her bed, and could not take it any longer. In a burst of anger she reached down and grabbed the frog firmly in her fist and hollered, "Now you will be quiet you horrible frog!" and threw him against the wall with a mighty **SMASH**.

But when he fell he was no longer a frog but a handsome young prince with kind and beautiful eyes.

The king was happy as the two were wedded for life.

The prince told how a wicked witch had turned him into a frog and that only a princess could release him.

That morning, as the golden sun cast its rays upon the land, a coach drawn by eight white horses in golden harnesses with white feathers upon their heads drove up to the castle. At the rear of the coach stood Faithful Henry, the loyal servant of the prince. Faithful Henry had been so deeply saddened by the spell that turned his master into a frog that he had three bands of iron placed around his chest to keep his poor heart from breaking.

Faithful Henry lifted the pair into the carriage and took his place at its rear. As the carriage rolled away, the prince heard a loud cracking noise. He yelled to Faithful Henry that he was afraid something might be breaking. But Faithful Henry answered that it was simply the bands around his heart snapping free, now that the spell was broken and his master was free at last.

The End

Text adaptation copyright © 2007 Kathy-jo Wargin
Illustrations copyright © 2007 Anne Yvonne Gilbert

All inquiries should be addressed to:

MITTEN PRESS
An imprint of Ann Arbor Media Group LLC
2500 S. State Street, Ann Arbor, MI 48104

Printed and bound in China.

10 9 8 7 6 5 4 3 2 1

Library of Congress Cataloging-in-Publication Data
Wargin, Kathy-jo.
The frog prince / by the Brothers Grimm; as retold by Kathy-jo Wargin; illustrated by Anne Yvonne Gilbert.
p. cm.
Summary: As payment for retrieving the princess's ball, the frog exacts a promise which the princess is reluctant to fulfill.

ISBN-13: 978-1-58726-279-1 (hardcover: alk. paper)
ISBN-10: 1-58726-279-7 (hardcover: alk. paper)

[1. Fairy tales. 2. Folklore--Germany.] I. Grimm, Jacob, 1785-1863. II. Grimm, Wilhelm, 1786-1859.
III. Gilbert, Anne Yvonne, ill. IV. Frog prince. English. V. Title.
Pz8.W212Fr 2006
398.2--dc22
[E]
2006020283